TELL ME A STORY, MAMA

by *Angela Johnson*
pictures by *David Soman*

A TRUMPET CLUB SPECIAL EDITION

Published by The Trumpet Club, Inc.,
a subsidiary of Bantam Doubleday Dell Publishing Group, Inc.,
1540 Broadway, New York, New York 10036.
"A Trumpet Club Special Edition" with the portrayal of a
trumpet and two circles is a registered trademark of
Bantam Doubleday Dell Publishing Group, Inc.

ISBN 0-440-83261-6

This edition published by arrangement with Orchard Books.

Printed in the United States of America
September 1995
5 7 9 10 8 6 4
UPR

The text of this book is set in 16 point Pasquale Book.
The illustrations are watercolor paintings, reproduced in full color.

To my grandfather, who told stories.

—A.J.

To my mom and Max, for all their love and teaching.

—D.S.

Tell me a story, Mama, about when you were little.

What kind of story, baby?

Just any old story. How 'bout the time you lived in a little white house across the field from that mean old lady?

Meanest woman I've ever known, too, baby!

She was so mean that she used to holler out her window at you and Aunt Jessie when you passed her house every morning.

You weren't afraid of her, though.

No sir, I was not.

One day she scared Aunt Jessie so bad by letting her old bulldog out to bark at you all that Aunt Jessie cried all the way home.

You went back and threw mud on her white picket fence.

I sure had a temper...

Grandmama made you apologize, but she kissed you hard on the head and gave you an extra sweet roll after dinner that night.

Your grandmama makes the best sweet rolls!

Is Grandmama going to stay here forever, Mama?
Just stay here and be Grandmama
forever to me?

She won't be here forever, baby,
but long enough for you never to forget
how much she loves you.

Did Grandmama squeeze you tight when you were her little girl,
like she does me?

Uh-huh.

You were lucky, too, Mama.

Yes, I was.

Remember the time when you were little and you found that puppy with no tail by the side of the road?

Poor little thing…

You kept it hidden in your sweater, huh, Mama?

We had three dogs already.

You kept it hidden until it got hungry and started to cry.
Grandmama didn't say anything. She took that little puppy from you
and wrapped it up in her apron. She gave him milk and then
let him live in the milk crate with your old baby blanket.

From one baby to another, she said.

Do all animals have babies, Mama?

Yes they do, the females at least.

Puppies, huh?

No sir!

Aunt Jessie is the baby in your family.

Yes, she is.

Why did Grandmama and Grandaddy send you and Aunt Jessie
off to St. Louis when you were both younger than me?
Alone, on a train?

They had to work. And your great-aunt Rosetta was lonely for children.
Hers were all grown up. Jessie and me, we kept her company
for a few months.

Did your mama and daddy miss you?

Like you'd miss the sun, baby. We missed them, too,
but we loved Aunt Rosetta.

Aunt Jessie cried when the train pulled out of the station and you couldn't see Grandmama and Grandaddy anymore.

She cried all over me!

It's all right to cry, though. Right, Mama?

If you feel like it, it's okay.

I feel like it sometimes, like when my best friend Cory moved away.
I did cry then. I bet Cory cried, too.

I'll bet he did.

Would you cry if I moved away, Mama?

Yes, I will…

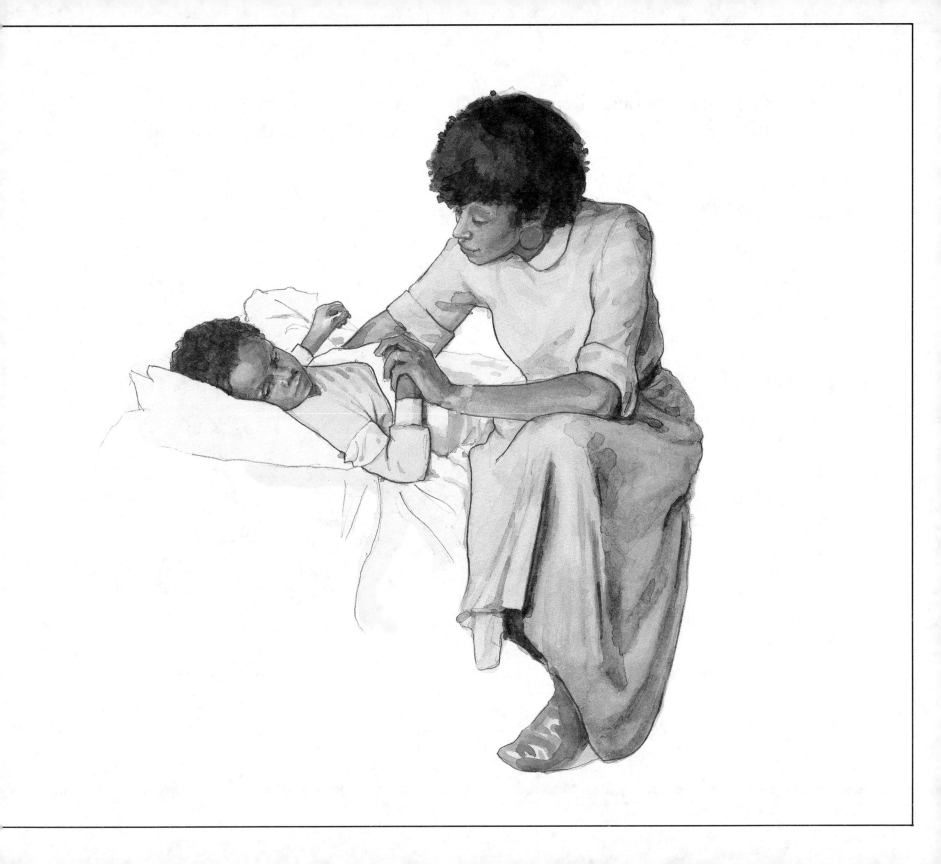

Grandmama cried when you moved away, Mama. She cried so hard that everybody at the airport looked at her and Grandaddy bought her flowers and a candy bar.

I remember.

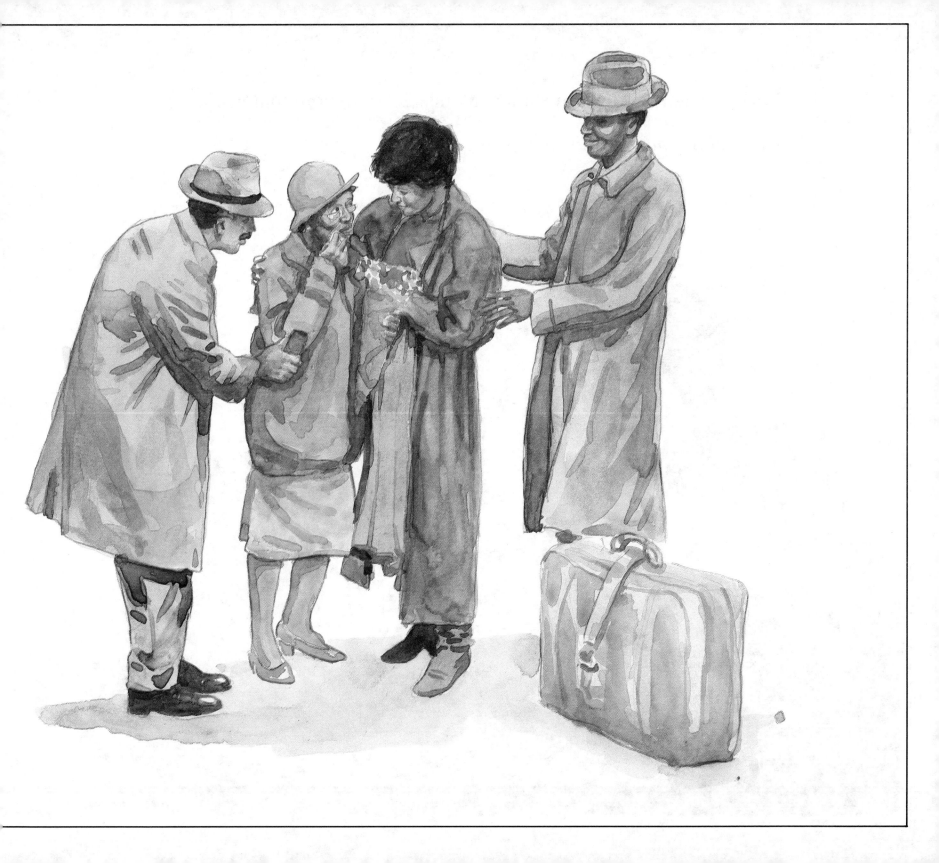

I like it when you tell me stories, Mama. Tell me more tomorrow.

Okay, baby. More stories tomorrow.